MAKING of THE BOSS

VIKAS MAHALA

BLUEROSE PUBLISHERS
India | U.K.

Copyright © Vikas Mahala 2024

All rights reserved by author. No part of this publication may be reproduced, stored in a retrieval system or transmitted in any form or by any means, electronic, mechanical, photocopying, recording or otherwise, without the prior permission of the author. Although every precaution has been taken to verify the accuracy of the information contained herein, the publisher assumes no responsibility for any errors or omissions. No liability is assumed for damages that may result from the use of information contained within.

BlueRose Publishers takes no responsibility for any damages, losses, or liabilities that may arise from the use or misuse of the information, products, or services provided in this publication.

For permissions requests or inquiries regarding this publication, please contact:

BLUEROSE PUBLISHERS
www.BlueRoseONE.com
info@bluerosepublishers.com
+91 8882 898 898
+4407342408967

ISBN: 978-93-5611-259-9

Cover Design: Muskan Sachdeva
Typesetting: Pooja Sharma

First Edition: September 2024

Preface

In 2028, one of India's significant business tycoons, recently acquired an international cricket team of India which he is captaining himself. It's about a person whose courage was bigger than the whole universe. He proved to the world that nothing is impossible. He showed the world that, a man can achieve anything by hard work and dedication.

This is a story of a sportsman, who then becomes a Business Tycoon. And then after becoming a Business Tycoon, he achieves his dreams of becoming a sportsman. This novel is based on a man who shows resilience and a 'never giving up' attitude.

The story sheds light on the events of how an ordinary farmer and the son of a laborer goes from rags to riches.

I dedicate the completion of this story to my friend Rakesh Bera, Mr. Ravikumar, and Banwari for providing their unmatched support.

All characters and events in this story are fictional andany resemblance to a person living or dead is purely coincidental.

VIKAS MAHALA

Date: 28th February, 2028 (The auction for buying the team franchises for Indian Cricket Council (ICC) is being held in Taj Hotel, Mumbai.)

K.K (Kamal Kishore) along with his partner R.K (Rakesh) was waiting in the lobby for the bidding of Rajasthan Tigers to start.

R.K- Brother (K.K) what do you think? Will this Sumit Modi let us take the franchise easily?

K.K- Don't you worry. Your brother can handle everything.

(The bidding starts)

Organizer- The bidding will commence from 600 crores as it's the base value of Rajasthan Tigers. Last year this franchise was bought for 580 crores. But this year, the base price is kept 600 crores by ICC, so let's start from there.

Sumit Modi- 630 crores from my side.

Alok Dalmia- 635 crores from me.

Sumit- 650 crores!

Dhiraj Kapoor- I bid 680 crores.

Sumit- 700 crores.

Dhiraj Kapoor- 750 crores from me.

Sumit: 900 crores!!

(The hall is silent)

Organizer- Is there any bid higher than 900 crores? 900 crores going once, going twice......(Meanwhile, K.K gestures to R.K)

R.K- 1100 crores!!

(Everyone in the hall begins to look at recent bidder, and whisperings start as to who is crazier than Modi about this team.)

Person sitting in the hall- Don't you know him; he is the director of the India's biggest upcoming Export Company.

Organizer- Is there any bid higher than 1100 crores? 1100 crores going once, going twice, going thrice and SOLD!! The owners of Rajasthan Tigers are men of the Boss Export, Mr. K.K and R.K.

(Everybody congratulates them.)

In the Media Conference:

Reporter- Mr. R.K, you bought the R.T franchise with such a high bidding, any special reason?

R.K- I had the authorization from my brother so he will tell you the reason.

(K.K had the looks and personality of a superstar. With 6ft height, muscular physique, he was always dressed in t-shirt and jeans. His strong and macho biceps could be seen from the t-shirt. His killer smile made him all the more attractive. He was tall, dark and handsome making him a perfect man.

On the contrary R.K could always be spotted in three-piece suits, with a passion for fancy clothing and luxurious cars. With a height of 5.9ft with a fair complexion similar to that of a foreigner, it was difficult to tell believe him an Indian. He had an extremely attractive personality.)

Reporter- Yes K.K, please tell us the reason for buying the team with such high bidding.

K.K-(smiling softly), Somethings are priceless and I am a businessman, I won't make a bad deal.

R.K- Okay thankyou everyone. We have to leave due to an important meeting.

(R.K and K.K leave the conference hall. And in their Rolls Royce parked in front of the hotel they go away)

K.K- Raku, how many times I have told you that you have to answer all the questions of the reporters, still you drag me in the middle of it.

R.K- (Smiling) Brother, you know I don't have such professional skills. I am only a technical guy.

I have done the work that you told me to do. You know there isn't anything that you have told me to do and I failed.

(The car stopped at the VIP gate of the Mumbai Airport, where the Airport staff ushered them towards their Private Jet. After a while the Jet took off towards a small town called Kishangarh.)

In the plane:

R.K- Brother, we definitely have to take Viraj Kohli in our time. He is my favorite player.

K.K- His days are over, that new boy Vishnoi plays well. And I know you want to take Viraj only because of that actress Tanishka. You won't change.

R.K- We'll take Vishnoi too but please, we have to take Viraj, you know how badly I want him on our team.

K.K- At his rate, we can get three other better players. But its fine, we'll take him as I can't say no to you.

R.K- (smiling) Okay.

K.K- When is the auction for the players Raku?

R.K- Brother it's on the 18th of the next month.

(Plane lands after an hour in Kishangarh)

(Next day the newspaper headline reads "The highest bid in the history of Indian Cricket by the Boss Export")

R.K- Brother, who will be captaining our team? Shall we keep the last year's captain AgaR.Kar, and also the coach Mr. Joshi? What do you think?

K.K- We'll appoint a new player as a captain.
R.K- Who?

K.K- Mr. Joshi is fine as a coach, but I'll be captaining the team.

R.K- I know very well that you don't drink, neither do you have any kind of addictions. A captain is the one who leads with his attitude and set an example by his play for other players. And your age is 43, it's been 20 years since you played. If this is a joke, let's just end this conversation here.

K.K- I am not joking Raku. I am quite serious about this and I have been practicing since the last six months for this.

R.K- Brother I know that you were a very good player in your time but this is an International Tournament, not some Gully Cricket. People will make fun of our company too along with you.

K.K- Do you trust your brother or not?

R.K- 100 percent brother!

K.K- If I fail in any aspect of batting, bowling or fielding from your Viraj, Vishnoi or those two players from Indies, I will not captain the team or be a part of it.

R.K- Now that's more like a man.

(I was thinking that once my brother intends to do something, he surely accomplishes it. And in our town, people leave their bats and run away when he starts bowling.

Standing and bowling at such a high speed, with in-swing and out-swing both, that too wicket to wicket. His bowling was the other name of evil in our district of Marwad. No one has hit a six till date, while he bowled.

It has been years since these miracles. But as far as I know, my brother has magic in his hands. In whichever field he has gone, the world has come to his feet.

He always came to open, and the record for hitting the longest sixes is still in his name in Marwad. He bats with both right and left hand, has a strike rate of more than 200 by both.

(Meeting with Mr. Joshi before the auction of the players.)

Mr Joshi was a retired Test player of the Indian Cricket. He is known for his strictness and discipline. His famous dialogue is "The one who doesn't have control over himself, can never control a bat or ball". He is a respectful member of the Indian cricket.

In the meeting hall:

(Team's coach: Mr. Joshi, Team's manager: Mr. Adams, Bowling coach: Mr. Prasad are all present. As soon as K.K and R.K enter, everyone stands.)

R.K- This isn't necessary.Please sit, as you are all valuable members of our team. Please meet the new owner of the team. We have decided to retain you all for this session of the ICL.

We have called this meeting to discuss about some necessary changes, that will be done after your approvals. "Over to you Mr. Joshi".

Joshi- First of all I would like to thank you for retaining us, and letting us be a part of this team.

K.K- We haven't given a chance to you, it's all because of your skills and talent Mr. Joshi.

Joshi- In my opinion team should have a mixture young and experienced players both, so I would suggest you to focus on these players in the auction.

(Handed the list to K.K)

R.K- Okay, as you'll be in the auction you can see it accordingly. And what do you think about the captainship? As Mr. AgaR.Kar has retired from all formats of the cricket, so whom should we appoint as a captain.

(As soon as I said this, brother started watching me like a little boy in need of his favorite toy.)

Joshi- Pawar will be suitable for captain ship. In my opinion, he is immensely talented and has shown great potential. And also, he has been the former captain of RT.

R.K- I agree with you. But we should appoint someone who is a real leader and a s sportsman.

Joshi- Whom are you suggesting?

R.K- My brother, Mr.K.K.

Joshi- (Smiling) If this is a joke, it's really nice.

R.K- I am very serious Joshi Ji.

Joshi- (In a serious tone) This is not some Gully Cricket. R.K Sahab, this is an international cricket tournament. People will laugh at us. I am sorry, but I do not agree with you at all. I am the coach of this team. You can buy cricket teams from money, but not the cricketing skills. If you want me to coach this team, I can't allow this at all.

K.K- (Calmly) Joshi I completely agree with you, but you haven't watched my play. You can't make up your mind without testing someone. I request you to watch my play first and if you think I am not capable of playing, I'll not insist you.

Joshi- Okay then, meet me tomorrow morning in the stadium. Let's see what you can do.

K.K- Thank you for giving me a chance. Let's meet tomorrow morning.

(To everyone) Okay, you can all go.

(After everyone leaves, in the lobby)

Joshi- What does this K.K think of himself. Tomorrow morning he'll know his place, that this all is not a joke.

Bowling coach Prasad- Yes Joshi ji. we'll see this businessman tomorrow.

(Meanwhile, in the meeting room)

K.K- (thinking himself) You know what you are capable of, just trust yourself and the practice you did for the last six months. Let's see tomorrow.

Tomorrow morning in the SM Stadium, Kishangarh:

Joshi- So tell me Mr. K.K, which aspect of cricket is your forte.

K.K- I am an all-rounder.

Joshi- Okay then start bowling, I'll bat.

(In the nets)

Joshi was a great player in his time, with a strong defense. He wore the pads and stood near the wicket and said to K.K, "Go Ahead!".

K.K- (Positioning himself straightly, with the ball in his hand like a fast bowler. With a run-up of just four steps, lesser than the run-ups of spinners nowadays.)

Joshi- (Calling out loudly) Are you bowling spin?

K.K- That you'll know in a few seconds sir. You can see for yourself.

(With that K.K moves into his bowling action and in front of the wicket, with right arm over the wicket, he throws the ball. The ball was of good length and pitched at leg stump and with a little swing, struck right at the off stump!!

Joshi was bowled out at the very first ball.

Joshi- It was the fastest leg cutter that I've faced in all my life. (Calls out Prasad) Please check and tell me, what was the speed of this ball?

Prasad- It was 141km/hr.

Joshi- (Impressively to Prasad) Such great speed, with a short run-up. Check his bowling action for any inaccuracies.

Joshi- (to K.K) Yes, please continue.

(This time bowling coach was looking at K.K's bowling action and run-up quite carefully. With a short run-up, he again threw the ball of good length, leg stump delivery and straightaway it struck on the pads in front of the wicket.

Joshi was out again by LBW. Out twice on two balls!

Joshi gestured to Prasad, inquiring about the bowling action)

Prasad- Perfect.

Joshi- (to K.K) Throw the next ball.

(This time it was a yorker that struck straight on the heel of the right toe, which Joshi stopped somehow, almost losing his balance.

Now Joshi, went to the corner to talk to Prasad and then said "Do you want to test him?")

Prasad- Yes Mr. K.K, I am making a circle with chalk on the pitch. You have to pitch the ball in the circle, and have to make it swing both ways.

(Joshi was looking at all of this carefully and said to K.K)

Joshi- Where were you, for all this while my brother? Why didn't you try for the Indian Team? I have faced almost all the legendary bowlers, but you Mr. K.K are quite different and superior to all.

K.K- Should I show you my batting too, Sir?

Joshi- Leave the batting, I can tell the player's skills from afar. I shouldn't have talked like that with you in the meeting. I am really sorry for that. We shouldn't judge anyone before knowing them.

(Everybody congratulated K.K)

K.K- I liked your attitude Mr. Joshi, nobody apart from you would have the told the team owner as it is. Let's meet at the reserve player auction now.

Date: 18th March 2028, Reserve player auction at the Taj Hotel, Mumbai.

(Viraj Kohli's base price is 2 Crores.)

Alok Gupta- 2.50 crores.

R.K- 3 Crores!

Alok- 3.5 Crores from me.

R.K- 4 Crores.

Alok- 5 Crores.

R.K- 6 Crores!

Alok-6.5 Crores.

K.K- Raku what are you doing, let him go.

R.K- No brother, you don't know. I am his big fan. And, my favorite actress will also come with him.

K.K- (Rolling his eyes) Oh, so that's the matter.

R.K- 7 Crores.

Organizer- In 7 Crores. Viraj is of RT's.

K.K- Happy now? From 2 to 7!!

(After the bidding ends, the team is as follows:

1. K.K (Kamal Kumar) Captain
2. Viraj Kohli
3. Hemant Vishnoi
4. Dharmesh Sangha (Wk)
5. Nawab
6. Saddam
7. Hafiz
8. Maxtell
9. Ben Stoff
10. Prem Chopra
11. Sumit Godara
12. Vikas Yadav
13. Jofra Komp

R.K- Brother, a mail has come from India Daily News. They want to take your interview. What should I say Sunday morning?

K.K- Tell them at 9.

R.K- Okay brother.

(R.K sends the mail that appointment is fixed at Boss's House, Village Kishangarh.)

At the India daily office in Mumbai:

We have to go to Rajasthan for K.K's interview.

"He is such a big businessman and still lives in a village. He has about 500 offices in more than 180 countries, still he operates from a village. There is the head office.

Neha – Ok so when do we have to go?

"Leave on Saturday as the appointment is on Sunday."

(Neha at the K.K's Mansion on the Sunday morning)

Neha- good morning Mr. K.K.

K.K-Good morning. What will you have tea, coffee or lassi?

Neha- You can call me Neha sir. Tea is fine.

K.K- Ok. Kalu Kaka! please bring some tea for the lady.

Neha- So shall we start the interview?

K.K- Yes of course.

Neha- Sir, you live in this village and your head office is also situated here. Is there any specific reason for this, even though all the multinational companies have their offices in metropolitan cities?

K.K- I love this place and I believe that business doesn't come from Metropolitan cities but from the brains. And in today's time it's all about technology as everyone can work from their homes. Business centralization is more important.

Neha- A farmer's son from a small village is now one of the top 10 businessmen with no formal business background. How did you create such a huge Business Empire?

K.K- With pure honesty and hard work have I achieved everything today.

Neha- Tell me something about your past, how did you start this? Tell us from the beginning.

K.K- Okay I'll start from my childhood. I was a very shy kid and I also stammered a lot. My neighbors and friends at school made fun of me because I could not even say my name properly. But I was really sharp in Maths and Cricket. I used to get hundred on hundred in maths and in cricket I used to be man of the match every time. Everyone said that only my tongue stutters and not my hands or my brain.

Everywhere there were people who want to pull you down, similar to that there were people in my life who made fun of my stuttering voice.

Till I was a kid I did not care about it, but when I got into my teenage, I used to wonder why I could not speak like normal people. But there was one person who thought that I was perfect and that was my mother.

My mother was a simple lady. She used to get sad in other people's sadness and happy in other people's happiness.

She used to say that I was perfect. I don't know why she thought that, because all the other people thought that I was good for nothing as I could not even speak.

Neha- Then how did your voice came back?

K.K- I went to a speech specialist in Jaipur for counselling for the duration of 20 days. Then after years of hard work my stammering stopped.

The doctor told me one thing that stayed with me. It was that I am unique. I am a hero and not a loser.

I was in 12th standard at that time. The next time when I entered school I was a hero and I believed only that.

But still some bullies at school used to trouble me, for them I was that old weak kid.

They had a whole group named Eagle group with their leader Gaurav, from whom everyone feared and I had just one friend named Amit, who was a naive kid like me.

One day when we were playing cricket, I bowled him a bouncer that struck straight on his helmet.

He lost his balance and fell on the ground. Then his whole group surrounded me.

Gaurav how dare you bowl me a bouncer don't try to be like Ambrose. Your wrists are very fast. After saying this he held me by my collar. I said to him that if he wants to see my strength let's have a one-on-one fight. If you beat me now with 10 other kids, it's not as if you will win the World Cup. After hearing this he said to me "You will fight with me, the school's boxing champion?"

When I challenged him for a fight, he became mad thinking that a loser boy like me was challenging him.

He agreed and asked me, "Where do you want to fight?".

I said "You decide the place and time but the fight will be only between us and nobody should come in between."

He agreed by saying that we will go to the vacant bungalow behind the school. I went along with Gaurav and his 10 friends. But I had decided in my mind that I will make him pay today.

I had Amit with me too, he told me to go home and avoid this fight. I thought in my mind if I did not fight today, I will never be able to fight from any challenge in my whole life. I was tired of running from my fears.

We came to the compound of the vacant bungalow and Gaurav was pretty confident about him winning this fight. I made a circle from a stick and said to Gaurav, "The fight will not be over till either I will beg you to stop it, or you will beg me to stop it". One of the friends of Gaurav said to me that "You better beg now".

In the circle:

I stared deep into Gaurav's eyes and punched him straight in the jaw. He fell on the ground. I started kicking him madly and his mouth started bleeding. In the whole fight I was winning. He was almost knocked out and then he held my feet to stop.

After that, I straight away picked up my bag and went home with Amit.

Till the next day the whole school knew about how K.K had won, in a fight with Gaurav.

When i came to school the next day, I thought that I had entered some other school as everybody was calling out my name respectfully, as K.K brother. And the kids who were troubled by Gaurav came to congratulate me saying, "You have done well". Now I was the new don of the school. Now everybody came to me about their problems even before the principal. This incident termed me as a fighter. It gave me the courage to fight all my battles.

Neha- How did you come into business?

K.K- Because of cricket.

Neha- Because of cricket? I do not understand.

K.K- It's a long story.

Neha- Please tell me sir, I want to hear it.

K.K- I was a champion bowler and batsman of my town and in state level tournaments I was always among the top ten. No batsman had ever hit a six on my bowling, and at the time I was only 17.

At that time ICL tournament was getting organized in India for the very first time. The selection committee of the team Rajasthan Tigers, had come to Jaipur for recruiting young players.

I took my certificate and cricket kit for the registration. A former player of the Indian team was there for team selection. He took my trial and shortlisted me and had called me the next day.

I felt like I was on cloud nine due to my happiness. The next day the selector called me and told me that I was very talented and that my bowling and batting was world class. He said, "We would like to give you a chance",

I said, I was forever indebted to them for this chance.

Selector-But everything comes with the price, which you have to pay. Arrange a sum of 15 lacs, so that the next process can start.

K.K -15 lacs sir? You told me that I was a brilliant player.

Selector- In India, this type of chance is given to a very few people. You have one week to arrange the sum and give it to my assistant. This is his number. Listen boy, millions of people play cricket in India, but this chance has only come to you.

K.K- Sir I am a farmer's son. I don't have such a huge amount of money.

Selector- If you are a farmer's son then do farming, because cricket costs money.

K.K- Please sir, you have seen me play.

Selector- Dozens of boys like you are waiting, we have to think about ourselves to. If you can manage the money, good. If not then I will choose someone else. After saying this he went to his car and left.

In my village I never thought about money because of the abundance of good food, lots of milk and polite people.

I took the bus and returned from Jaipur.

The whole night I kept thinking about how should I ask my mom and dad who were just simple farmers about such a big sum of money. I had never even asked 100 rupees from them till now. Because they were against me playing cricket, and wanted me to study and become a teacher. If I shared the talks of 15 lakhs with them, they would have given me 15 spankings.

The next day my neighbor Raku came to me who is my business partner now. He was eight years old at that time and learnt cricket from me.

Raku- Brother where are you?

K.K's mother- He is still sleeping.

(Raku coming into K.K's room)

Raku- Brother please wake up. Let's play cricket.

K.K- I am not in the mood today.

R.K- How was your trial for Rajasthan tigers they surely selected you didn't they, now we will see you live on tv.

After hearing this my eyes started watering.

R.K-What happened brother why are you crying?

K.K- Raku, they asked for money for my selection.

R.K- That's why you are crying? Don't worry brother I have lots of money in my Piggy Bank, just take it all and give it to them.

After hearing this from a little kid I thought that, at least there is one person who is with me.

K.K- No idiot, they have demanded lots of money that probably the whole village doesn't have.

R.K- Is money everything brother?

K.K- It's not everything but it is something. If you have money, you can do anything.

R.K- Then I think you should earn money brother and buy the whole freaking team which you can captain one day.... My mother is calling me I should go home.

K.K- You have said rightly kid. I will earn money and buy a whole team of ICL. I will not marry before completing this goal and neither will I ever sleep in a bed till then.

This is my solemn pledge that I want to earn enough money that every wish of mine comes true. I had pledged this but now I actually had to make money. I thought of talking to my mother about this.

Maa- I have made roti and also your favorite kheer. My lovely son will become healthy, then only he will score long sixes.

K.K- I don't want to scores sixes I want to earn money.

Maa- (smiling) Eat this roti first and after that you can earn as much as you want.

K.K- I will not eat roti just tell me first how to earn lots of money.

Maa- Son by working in the fields you can earn hundred rupees daily, but if you learn to read and write and become a teacher then you can earn 500 rupees daily, and if you become an officer, you can earn 1000 rupees daily. Now you can think how much you want to earn.

K.K-I don't want to earn hundred 500, 1500. I want to earn 1 crore rupees.

Maa- One crore rupees daily! Have you gone mad? Oh God what has happened to my son!! Has anyone done black magic on him?

K.K- Just tell me how to earn this much money. Isn't there anyone in India who earns this much money daily?

Maa- This much money is only earned by Tata, Birla and Ambani.

K.K- If they can earn this much then why can't we?

Maa- They are big men. They got money from their ancestors too.

K.K- What do they do, that they earn so much money?

Maa- They are businessman. They do business.

It has immense possibilities to earn money. Their fathers and forefathers were businessman but we are just farmers.

K.K- So that means to earn money you have to do business?

Maa- Yes but not just that, it takes some investment to start a business which we do not have and neither do you have any experience. So that's why I am saying, just eat your food and take care of the farm as nowadays wild animals are ruining our crops.

K.K- I will not go to college. From tomorrow I will do my studies from private and I will start a business.

Maa- Oh God what has happened to you? If you will not study, how will you get a job?

K.K- I will give other people jobs ma, don't you worry!

Maa- Ok then eat your food, and then you can do your business.

There was an old friend of mine in my class his name was also Gaurav. His father was in oil business and his house was nearby to mine so I went to his house to ask his father for work.

K.K- Uncle please keep as a worker in your factory.

Manak ji- Aren't you Bhawar's kid? You are famous for Maths and cricket in the village.

Boy you should study right now, you can do the small jobs anytime.

K.K- No sir I need to work and I am continuing my studies through private.

Manak ji- Which work do you know?

K.K- Whatever you will say sir from accounts to labor. It will take a little time but I will learn everything.

Manak ji- How much salary do you want?

K.K- You can decide whatever you think is worthy after seeing my work.

Manak ji- OK then, you can come from tomorrow onwards.

First day of the job:

(Manak ji to the accountant), "he has come, explain him the work and send him along with the supply truck from tomorrow"

Accountant- Ok sir.

Accountant to K.K- This is an oil business which is sent to factories and used for automobiles. From tomorrow, you have to go with the driver for delivery. For today, I will give you some knowledge about the products that we work with.

K.K- Ok sir.

So hence I learnt about the supply work in 15 days and in three months I even increased their sales.

Manak Sir promoted me and made me the head of sales in the office.

One day Manak sir was searching for a Maths tuition teacher for his daughter.

Manak to accountant- May daughter Vaishali is in 10th standard, let me know if you have any good Maths teacher in mind who can come home and teach her.

Accountant- Sir our K.K is a topper in Maths. He gets hundred on hundred, surely, he will teach your daughter.

Manak sir looked at me and said "you should come in the evening to our house K.K and teach Maths for an hour to Vaishali".

"I will pay you separately for that."

K.K- I am not a professional teacher sir, if she has any problems in Maths that I can explain her.

The next day I told my mother that I will come a little late in the evening as I have to tutor Manak sir's daughter.

Next day in the evening I went to Manak Ji's house, his wife opened the gate and I greeted her.

Wife- Oh yes Vaishali's father told me that you are going to come. Wait let me make tea for you and then she called Vaishali.

"Vaishali your Maths sir has come!"

Vaishali- Yes mummy, I am coming please ask him to wait.

Vaishali was a beautiful girl with blue eyes and she was almost 15. She was wearing a blue colored skinny jeans with a fitted t-shirt when she came into the room. We introduced ourselves to each other.

Her mother entered with tea and snacks and said to me "She has been failing in Maths. From the last two years she has been in the 10th class. Please do whatever you can so that she passes this class."

K.K- It's no problem aunty, I will try my best and of course she also has too.

This was my daily routine now after office I came to her house to teach her.

Vaishali was also trying her best and focusing ln studies. But she often came closer to me while I was teaching. She found ways of touching me or my hair to flirt with me. Whenever I taught her, her eyes stayed on my face more than the books. But I ignored this even though, I noticed everything and just sticked to my job.

One day her parents were both gone out and were to come late in the evening. Sir called me in the phone saying that they'll be a little late.

Vaishali had ditched her normal jeans and t-shirt today for a mini- skirt.

As soon as I entered, she smiled and said "Come sir I'll serve you tea from my own hands today" and went into the kitchen to make tea. She came back two minutes later with two cups of hot tea and served it.

K.K- Vaishali yesterday I gave you an exercise of trigonometry. Did you do it or not?

Vaishali- Sir at least finish the tea first.

And then she sipped her tea. After two sips, in a hurry she spilled the tea on my clothes.

"I am so sorry there was a cockroach".

K.K- Its Ok.

Vaishali- Please unbutton your shirt and give it to me.

I refused her saying I'll clean it at home.

Vaishali- I will not study until you give me your shirt.

I unbuttoned my shirt and gave it her while facing the other side.

As soon as I did that, she held me from behind and hugged me. I pushed her back and said "What are you doing".

Vaishali- I really love you!

K.K -Have you gone mad I am your teacher. There isn't any love in a student-teacher relationship.

Vaishali- Yes, I have become mad in your love. This is such a conservative thinking. Today everything is acceptable.

K.K- Maybe it's acceptable for you city folks, but for us village people, our rules and principles are very important. And one more thing we don't bite the hand that feeds us. I will never break your father's trust.

And the love that you are talking about is only lust. Love is only from heart. Lust can only satiate the body's hunger.

And madam my pants aren't so loose as to open anywhere. And if you love me truly, control yourself and your body and just focus on your studies. I am very far from any kind of physical attraction. My goals are different.

Vaishali- Just stop your lecture. If you will not accept my love, I'll ask my father to fire you. I'll defame you by saying that you harassed me when you found out I was alone.

K.K- I expected this from you. You are not in your senses right now. Gold will remain gold, it will not become copper if you say so.

I am going.

After saying that I left her house.

So, in this way I rejected my first love proposal.

On the next day:

K.K to Manak ji- I won't be able to teach Vaishali from now sir.

Manak ji- After so much has happened, still you had the guts to come here. Just go away from here and never show me your face again or else I'll call the police.

K.K- It was not my fault sir. Your daughter forced herself on me which I immediately refused.

Manak- You are putting the blame on my daughter? How dare you! You bastard. If I wasn't afraid of the insult in the society, I would have handed you over to the police. Why are you standing here? just get out of my face. Never come back again.

(I understood that Vaishali had taken her revenge. I became extremely depressed and went towards my home.

After coming home, I went to my room and cried in my pillow. I said to God, "I am not upset because I got fired, I am sad because of the shameful way they had treated me". But then I thought if I am not wrong why should I be sad? God has justice for everyone.

Maa- Son you came home early, are you alright?

K.K- Yes, I am fine. But I left my job.

Maa- What's there to be upset about? And also, you don't want to do a job remember, you want give other people jobs.

Now go and help in the farm for the harvest.

I always liked working in the field and to overcome this sadness I happily obliged. There is a saying that "For good people if one-way closes, the second one opens up automatically by God's grace".

My first business idea was given to me by a thief and that also is a wonderful story.

I was reading the paper in the morning. A News showed that police had arrested a gang of local boys stealing electric wires, oil of the transformers and other electrical equipment.

The material from the theft had been confiscated from the diesel tanker of their tractors.I was shocked to find out that they kept the power oil in the diesel tankers as I didn't know that it is beneficial for the diesel too.To find out answers about these questions I went to my friend who was a Diesel Mechanic."Usman bhai how are you?"."I am well by God's grace.""You tell K.K brother nowadays I'm not seeing you in the market. Where have you been?""Right now I am at home, I just wanted to get some information from you.Can this power oil be substituted in the place of diesel?""Brother, some people do run tractors and old pumps by this power oil, but it isn't very well available in the market.And now electrical pumps have come in the new cars and vehicles.It isn't as successful in them. It can be worked in tractors because their Diesel tank is located above. The power oil is a little denser than diesel. But I don't know the long term effect of this.""Thank you so much Osman brother you really helped me".Now I knew one thing that this can be used instead of diesel, but only for tractors and old vehicles.The only question was that, where should I get it from and that too in large quantity.I have done trade in oil that's why I knew some factories in Jaipur who filtered the old oil.In our tongue we called them black oil filter refineries.Next day, I left for Jaipur and went to the refinery straightaway.I went to meet the production manager."Sir do you have an availability of old power oil?""Yes, we do arrange auctions for Electrical oil of the power house.""Can you give me the filtered power oil?""For that you would have to talk to the owner of the factory Mr Modi. I am giving you his number you can talk to him. Actually, he is going to come here in a while, you could wait in the office."After an hour Mr Modi came to the office and asked the manager, "Who is this boy and if he has come for some job, tell him there is no vacancy".

Manager- No sir he has come to buy the electric power oil, I asked him to wait for you.Modi- OK then send them inside.K.K-Greetings Mr Modi my name is K.K and I am from Kishangarh.Modi-Tell me what can I do for you?K.K- Sir I need filtered power oil, if you can give it to me please provide me the rates.Modi- Yes sure, you can take it in whichever quantity you want.For you the rate will be 36 rupees per litre and additional 18 percent with bill. Without the bill its 9 percent but risk of taking the oil will be up to you.K.K- Without bill? I do not understand.Modi- I mean without bill you will get a profit of 9%.What's the name of your firm by the way?K.K- Right now, I do not have the registration of the firm I am 3 months short to complete 18 years of age.Modi- You are a child right now in the trade, and you do not have any experience too.Son I think you should start your firm first and then think about the raw material.K.K- No Mr. Modi, the firm will open soon but right now I need four drums of 200 litres of oil.Modi- Ok you can take it at your own risk, the drums will cost you 32000 rupees. Please pay it to the cashier. You can take the oil from the factory but if the sales tax people catch you we will not be held responsible.K.K- Ok Modi ji. I will take the oil tomorrow.

Modi to manager Mishra- What do you think will this kid buy the oil?Manager- That we will know tomorrow sir.K.K- How will I arrange 32000 rupees till tomorrow I should ask my mother, as she is my only bank."Maa I need to talk to you"Maa- Tell me what happened?K.K- I need 32000 rupees.Maa- Why, what for?K.K- I am going to start a new business so I need to buy material for it.Maa- You are starting a new business and telling me just now, when you need the money.You have really grown mature.K.K- I was going to tell you maa, but everything happened in such a hurry I only had the time today.

Maa- I wouldn't have stopped you son, but you should have asked your father first.And then we would have asked Pandit Ji to tell an auspicious date to start the new business. Anyway, where have you seen the place for it?K.K- My innocent mother, I have been behind only because of waiting for approvals from everyone.Now I'll ask my father how should I do business and when should I start even though he is not a businessman?And as for Pandit Ji, do any foreigners take suggestions from Pandit Ji first before starting a business?My loving mother every day is auspicious if our intentions are pureI have just asked 32000 rupees. People spend at least a lakh to start a business.First renting a shop then arranging furniture. Here everything is happening in these 32000 rupees.Maa- Do you think I am an idiot? In today's time a vegetable cart will also be of more than 32000.K.K- I don't want to argue with you ma you know I have never asked for any money from father ever. Only you can help me. Just think like these 32000 rupees got lost for a while, please give me this much my loving mother.Maa- Ok do not butter me any more now. Take out 35000 from the cupboard I am loaning it to you and will take it back with 2% interest.K.K- You are the best mother in this whole world. You always take care of me.(Now I thought how will I get the oil from there.)Brothers Tempo is free, after distributing milk in the morning. let me talk to him.Pappu who lived in our neighbourhood was a very happy and helpful person.K.K- Pappu bhai Ram Ram.Pappu- are K.K brother how did you think of me.K.K- brother I have to go Jaipur. I need your Tempo for getting four drums of oil.Pappu- When do you have to go?K.K- Today only.Pappu- I cannot go today, I have to take my buffaloes for mating.I think you can go alone.K.K- Brother I don't know how to drive a Tempo and I have never even driven one.Pappu- Nobody learns to drive from their Mother's Womb and you know how to drive a tractor.K.K- Yes I drive a tractor and sometimes take it in the City too.Pappu- So then you don't need to worry you can take the tempo by God's name and do not worry at all it is fully insured. These are the keys now go quickly.K.K- But what about the money?Pappu- Arre just pay for the oil.K.K-

But how much?Pappu- I will not take more from you as you are my brother.

I started the tempo and in around 10 to 15 km on the Jaipur highway I got used to driving it.In two hours I arrived at the factory and Mr Modi arranged to load the four drums on the tempo.Modi- You drove the tempo from so far away this was quite risky.K.K- You have to take risks to become something,Modi to Mishra ji- Load the four drums of 200 litres in the tempo and give him a rough bill.After the loading I started my journey towards my village. It took two hours for me to come to the factory, but three hours to go back because of the loading time.I reached till the evening, then unloaded the drums and left the tempo at Pappu bhai's house.Pappu- I hope there was no problem.K.K- not at all everything was good.Pappu- you are just like my brother so you can give 2000 rupees. K.K- But the oil was only of 800 rupees.Pappu- aree brother, the EMI of the tempo also comes and after the maintenance charges nothing is left for me so you have to give 2000rsK.K- Ok take 2008 is my fault that I did not set the rate earlier.Pappu- In the business you should always learn to fix the rate beforehand. Learn from the incidents that people can never be what they look or seem to be. Their true nature comes out only after the trade.Now I had got the oil and after adding all the miscellaneous charges it costed me around 43 rupees per litre. And, right now the rate of the diesel was 62 rupees per litre.So I should keep it 5 rupees less than the rate of diesel and start my trade to the village Tractors.

Next day

(At Mohan kaka's house)

Kaka- Ram Ram

Mohan Kaka- How are you K.K?

K.K- I am good. Kaka you are a big farmer with three tractors, I am sure you must be using a lot of diesel. I am offering you the rate lesser than diesel with equally good quality.

Mohan Kaka- What have you brought as the diesels alternative?
Earlier the grocery store had kerosene oil, we used it a lot but now it is not available.

K.K- I have power oil it can be used as an alternative to diesel in your Tractors.

Mohan Kaka- aree you will ruin the engine with it. Is power oil even an alternative to diesel?

K.K-Engine is related to the pump and if something happened to your pump I will return you all your money. Just use it once and if any loss happens you can take it from me

Kaka- ok if you are saying this much then I can try it. Give just 40 litres for now to try.

Kaka ji was my first customer. I did not even take money from him and gave the oil as a loan to try as he was a very reputed person in our village.

If he started using my oil then other people will follow him.

Next day

Mohan Kaka- K.K what have you given to me to put into my Tractors?

K.K (scared)- what happened Kaka was there any trouble in the machine?

Kaka- it has been morning to evening but this oil is not finishing.
Normally a full tank of diesel is used up for 20 beegha of the farm, I have done around 30 beegha till now and still it isn't finished.

K.K (with relief)- so that means it is profiting you.

Kaka- how much do you have and what rate are you going to give me?

K.K- Kaka you are my relative so I will give you the rate of 55 rupees per litre, it is 5 rupees lesser than diesel. For 4 drums it will cost you 44000rs.

Kaka- ok come home and take the money and then give me those four drums of oil and write down my order for 10 drums.

K.K- ok take these for now the rest I will send you. In this way I earned a pure profit of rupees 7200 on the first day of business. Now I knew that my product had potential to do well in the market and it has very little competition too.

I was the king of my area now I just had to tie up with lots of farmers because it was a fast-moving consumable good. The machine needs fuel daily.

Next day I rented a pickup truck from the city and went to Modi Ji's factory

K.K- Greetings Mr Modi I need 10 drums now.

Modi- son you can take hundred instead of 10. Only today the auction of power house has happened.The Stock of thousand drums is coming so you can take the material without any worries.

K.K- But I will pay you half right now you can take the leftover amount the next time.

Modi- it's ok we can gauge a man's talent once. You are a man for the long haul.But remember one thing if you want to be a successful Businessman remember to pay your dues on time.

K.K- trust me sir as soon as the material is reached there I will transfer it in your account the next day.

Modi- No I will not take any money without billing . When you will come you can give it to me.

K.K- Thank you so much.

Modi to Mishra ji-load ten drums in his truck and write down the rest in the account.

Now I had gotten my hands on a solid product with a supplier. The margin was also 20% which was quite nice.

Next day I gave the ten drums to kaka and the profit of 25,000 was earned.

For a person who did a job for 5000, for him earning 33000 in profit in 3 days was a huge thing.I bought an old bike in 20000 Rs and then went for the marketing of my product to nearby farmers.

I already started marketing and it was profiting from it. Five out of ten people were ordering from me.

In a little while I sold 150 drums in just a month.

The profit was 3,00,000 rupees in the first month.I returned 50,000 to my mother in place of the 35000Rs and she got really happy.

But delivering drums in the pickup truck was turning out to be costly.

So I bought a second-hand pickup truck of one lakh rupees which I drove myself.Because the vehicle was old every part of it made noise except for its horn.But it drew well on the road.

I was still trading with a rough Bill.

Without a proper bill, it meant that I was stealing the taxes from the government.But as I was young I feared no one.

I bought without bill and sold without bill, thinking who will get in the mess of paperwork and Taxes.

As I didn't know much about the filing of the firms paperwork.

My formula was working perfectly as people were demanding for my product more and more. It was sacred for Tractors and farmers were also profiting who were already in debt.

Like the daily routine I went to the factory to pick-up the delivery but my left eye was fluttering that day. I did not believe in good and bad luck so I ignored it.

Halfway through, the sales tax car with the blue light was standing there and they were checking the loaded vehicles.

They stopped my truck and asked me, "What is in the truck?"

I never knew how to lie so I told them, "it has power oil sir."

He said "show me the bill"

I said "I don't have the bill sir".

As soon I said this they surrounded me like I was some sort of a criminal.

He doesn't have the bill check how much material there is in the truck and seize the truck. As soon as he said this one man climbed on the truck and started checking the drums.

A person who looked like an officer to me I approached and greeted him.

Officer- from where are you taking this and where will you go tell me the names of both the firms. Do you not know that taking the material without bill is a financial crime? The penalty will be 11 Times.

K.K- Sir it has been a mistake please leave me.

Officer- the penalty will be at least 5 lakh and the case will also be made up against you. In which world are you living firstly and you are stealing taxes.

He gestured worker

Go with him in the truck and seize the truck including the material in it.

After hearing this, the man sat with me in the truck and told me to start it.

I was thinking in my mind that I am stuck now very badly how will I get out of this situation

I started the car and drove on the way which the worker told me.

Subordinate officer- Our officer is very strict he will take at least 5,00,000 rupees to let you go. Today was your bad day son.

I had a plan in my mind.

As soon as we passed the busy highway I turned my truck to a Dirt Road.

Subordinate officer- Why did you pull the truck down here.
K.K- I am having trouble in my stomach so I need to find a place to relieve myself.

Subordinate officer- You can go in the office, now go from here.

K.K- Sir it is not in my hands.

And I stopped the truck in the middle of the way.

There was no one near us only me and that subordinate officer.
He kept sitting in the car and I got out.

Subordinate officer- Do whatever you have to do fast.

I took out an iron rod from under the seat of the car and kept it on the bonnet in front of the truck.

And said to him in a deep voice "come out you dog, come out at once I will smash your head with this rod".

Slowly he came out of the truck in shock and said, "you are doing wrong.

Harming an on duty officer is a crime."

K.K- don't teach me the law I know all about the officers like you.

And took out 50000 rupees from my pocket and kept it on the bonnet.

And said to him, "choose one from these two. You have an option: if you want to get beaten then be prepared, No one will come to save you in the middle of this forest."

Subordinate officer- Ok give me the money I think it will be better" and he picked up the bundle of the notes as soon as he said it.

I held his hand and then said "wait brother why are you in such a hurry? Just tell me in front of the camera that I took 50000 rupees from K.K.

I don't trust you as you can take the money and also put a case as the number of the truck is with you."

Subordinate officer- No brother I cannot say in front of the camera if the video goes viral I will lose my job.

K.K- You value your job more than your life?

Speak in the front of the camera this instant or I will smash your head.

I said to him in a threatening tone and he agreed to say in front of the camera.

I gave him 50,000 rupees and started the truck.

Subordinate officer- At least leave me on the highway.

K.K- I am giving you 50,000 just call for a rented car.

And left him there leaving on the opposite road from my destination.

Somehow I had escaped this situation but I had learnt my lesson.

If I want to do a long term business it has to be done in a legal manner.

On the next day I went to the CA to start the registration of a new firm.

Now I had my legal firm with a small office in the City

Whatever material came, was with proper billing the profit was a little less but a self-relief was there, that I am not doing anything wrong.

Just like this the business expanded but it only worked in in the season of harvesting and cutting. Therefore, for six months there was an abundance of work, but then after calculating of a whole year the profit was of at least 18 to 20 lakhs.

Four years went by in this business and now I was in a better position in the village. My mother wanted to get me married. Maa- son I think now it's time for you to get married.Mr. Chaudhary of Ramgarh gave a marriage proposal of his daughter for you.They are big people you should at least see the girl once.

K.K- I think my mother is tired of coking and washing clothes for me.

Maa- yes beta at least assume this, that I want to play with my grandchildren now.

K.K- I will not get married for ten years I am only 23 now.

And regarding the cooking and cleaning, from tomorrow a maid will come.

Maa- In ten years the world will turn upside down, why are you troubling me so much? Please get married so that before I die, I can feed my grandchildren with my own hands.

K.K- Ask me any other thing instead of marriage.

Maa- Yes I know you have become a big person, you will not obey your mother, do whatever you feel like.

The time was fleeing. Six months work and six months rest.

I hated resting so I thought of trying my luck in some other business.

Soon that opportunity came up.

My friend was setting up a small factory of detergent powder I went there to check it out.Some chemical drums were there

I asked him "Vikram Bhai what comes in these drums?"

"Brother K.K there is chemical used for cleaning which is included in the Surf"

K.K- Vikram Bhai from where do these chemicals come?

Vikram- It is a great trouble. In Rajasthan, only two supplies are there. That too you have to send advance money, only then you can book for these chemicals.

K.K- And how many detergent factories are here?

Vikram- One factory is there in almost every district. Some demand 5 drums per month some ten or some twenty. It depends on their capacity.

When I talked to the suppliers who are in in the chemical manufacturing business, I got to know that there is a 25% profit in this business.

The demand is also good. Now I just have to look for potential consumers but this was not an easy task.

Because they were spread out in the whole state, so I thought of an idea.

I talked to Vikram's salesman who goes for delivery in almost half of Rajasthan.I said to him, "wherever you go there must be other local brands detergent you just have to get me 1 kg of each. For that I will pay you 200 per kg."

The idea worked and in 15 days I had a list of more than 30 local detergent brands and their mobile numbers.I just had to call everyone and I kept my price low.Ten deals were confirmed from the thirty.

And for their convenience I asked them to pay after the delivery.

The chemical was sold out within 5 days of getting it from the factory.

A direct profit of 3,00,000 rupees.

My hunger for earning money was increasing day by day.

My goals were not letting me sit in peace.

I was working hard day and night and now some savings were also accumulated.And as the saying goes your achievements depends on how big you dream.

The bigger you dream the more courage you have, to take action. And here I had gotten my heart broken by cricket. For the love of it I had to buy a whole freaking cricket team.

Now I had become a millionaire from rags to riches, but I wanted to become a billionaire, as for buying a team you need thousands of millions.

For a normal person this achievement was enough but I was still not satisfied.I kept thinking what I should do to achieve my dream that I saw those ten years back. The goal was almost like going to Mars.

Raku was older now and also the topper of his college. An 8 year old boy had become an adult.He had completed his graduation.

One day he came to me in the evening and said, "Brother I want to work for you, as in these times of inflation I cannot sit at home."

K.K- leave the job let's do business.

R.K- for that I need capital and experience which I do not have. I do not daydream.

K.K -which capital did I have Raku when I started my business from 35000 rupees and today I have a turnover of millions. You just need determination and an idea.

R.K- Not everybody is lucky like you that your business achieved great heights.

K.K- luck is just 1%, the other 99% is pure hard work. To achieve this much I only did hard work and was watchful of people around me.

Life gives everybody a chance, success only comes to those who take that chance. And destiny is also with them. Success only depends on our perseverance and the timing of the business.

Business and cricket both depend on timing if the timing is right even simple shots will reap you fours and sixes.

R.K- but I have nothing to invest in the business.

K.K- I don't want anything from you I just want you. You have a unique thing which only some possess from the thousands. That is honesty and truthfulness which is imperative to succeed.

I have seen you from your childhood and I know what kind of a man you are

You may be nothing for other people right now but from my eyes you are everything.

Do you remember ten years back you told me one thing when I was sad because I went unsold in the ICL. You told me "Brother just earn money and buy the whole cricket team".

I want my brother Raku along with me. Not working for me but with me as a business partner.

R.K- but brother....

K.K- I don't want to hear anything. From now you are my partner I have an idea in my mind which you will help me succeed in.

R.K- what is the idea?

K.K- there is an institute of 'Exports' in Ahmedabad, they have a course on import and export business of 3 months. You go there and learn how does the import business works.

R.K- but brother the business of export is huge and it happens in big cities.

People like us in small villages do not think about such huge business.

K.K- your brother is different from other people. My thinking starts from where other people's thinking ends. Only my tongue stutters not my hands and brains, you just get prepared to go to Ahmedabad.

R.K (smiling)- As you say brother.

Our relationship was very deep from the starting and now it has been ten years since I started a business. I had gotten plenty of experience and I knew that to do something big you need team work.

Just like how one batsman or bowler cannot win you World Cup the whole team's performance is important for that,Similarly to set up a huge business Empire you need a team I had learnt this from my 10 years of experience.

The goal that I want to achieve would need a whole team with proper planning.

Next day

R.K- brother I enquired about the institute we don't have to go to Ahmedabad for it.This course is available online and we can enrol in it while sitting at home that too in just 20,000. If I went to Ahmedabad, the stay alone for 3 months would cost around 20000, plus the added 20000 fees of the course.We'll save that money by enrolling online.

K.K- You have become a Businessman now in the very first time itself you have saved 20000 rupees of the company. This is called smart work by using the technology.I'm really impressed

Raku- Also brother you can take the course with me. One Enrolment free with one admission.

K.K- you'll achieve a lot raku you have hit a six on the very first ball.You are born for great things.

Raku- brother you are making fun of me now.

In this way me and Raku started taking the online course in the evening for 2 hours every day and started learning import and export.

-Slowly all our points cleared.

-How the shipping bills are made.

-How the payments are made.

-Which all Agencies can help us.

-Terms and conditions of the payments.

-And how the letter of credit is issued.

We collected lots of information by this course which we took in the evenings on our Ipads. The most important thing that we learnt was, just like soldiers are there on the boundaries of every Nation, similarly export is the economic soldier of a nation.

And by exports only the economic conditions of the nation can be improved.Collecting foreign currency for the nation increases the surplus of foreign currency. It balances the imports of the country and government also provides subsidies and different programmes to increase the number of Exports.But it was heart-breaking to know that our nation accounts for only 2% of all the export worldwide.

Whereas China's export percentage is 30%.

China and India's export were similar till 1990. But due to the change in the policies of China it became a world leader in export. And we left Behind stuck in pulling legs of each other.We are more knacky than these Chinese.

But because of lack of willpower and leadership, bad politics and corruption the economic condition of our nation is in ruins.

We have lack of information in today's time.

There are no programmes run by government for the encouragement of Exports. And even if there are, they are only for show.

The officers appointed in the import export unit are also those who have already worked in other departments. They have no experience about how to work in this field. They just make policies on paper, that too which are advantageous only for some handful of business families.

Only the trees who are big are watered. There is nothing done for the new saplings, those who dare to venture in this field. But now a farmer son has made up his mind to enter in this field.

I was determined to be a financial Soldier for our nation, as in the exports industry there are uncountable possibilities and opportunities.

In comparison to China, we have good quality material and the labor is also cheaper but because of lack of information our exports are affected by it. Me and Raku both completed our course together soon.

Once my driver of the pickup truck, took a leave for two days and there was an urgent delivery at a detergent factory. So, me and Rakesh went to the factory for delivery and took a payment of almost 3,00,000 rupees.

The way was quite long and at around 11 at night it started pouring heavily. The truck had slowed down because we could not see in front of us clearly. One car was following us for quite a while but I did not notice it.

K.K- Raku it's pouring heavily, I think we should stop the car and wait for it to slow down, I cannot see the road clearly.

R.K- Yes you are right just stop the car and switch on the parking light.

As soon as we stopped our car, the car following us came alongside with two men carrying pistols in their hands. They got out of the car as soon as I saw their weapons, I knew they were thieves and we were their prey for today so I started the car and raced it. They fired 3 rounds of bullets on us.

Raku- brother they are firing bullets.

A bullet almost came near to my ear and then passed to the windshield. The other two bullets got struck on the body of the pickup truck so I choose to take the truck on the highway.

Raku was very worried, he could not even speak, scared he asked me,

"What will happen now, will they kill us brother?"

K.K- Life and death is in God's hand if he has decided that today is our last day then nobody can stop it. But I cannot die like a coward. I will die fighting just tighten your seatbelt and trust God's will.

After this the thieves' car came alongside our truck. I bumped our truck from the right side with their vehicle just like they show in the movies. And for some time, we were ahead of them, but now they started aiming towards our tires and firing the bullets. I also started moving the truck like a snake in zigzag motion so that their aim is deterred.

By God's will all their aims missed every time. I pressed the break immediately when they were exactly behind us. Because of this their car bumped against our truck and the front part of it got damaged badly.

Taking a step ahead I shifted my truck in the reverse gear and smashed the truck in reverse onto their vehicle. I did this thrice to not give them any chance. When their car was damaged badly, I raced my pickup fast and accelerated. This time they did not follow us and we got out of this uninvited situation by our courage and will.

Raku was very much affected by this incidence said "brother today we both would have been exported from this world if not for you".

K.K- Only God has the power to give and take life. Even if death has come you should die fighting fearlessly and not hiding like cowards.

Raku (smiling)- Yes brother you told them that we are predators and not preys.

Next day:

Raku- brother what should we name the export?

K.K- Think of such a name that will impact people's heart and mind as soon as they hear it. It should be unforgettable. And also, it should get popular in the international market.

Raku- Only you can think of such a name.

K.K- How is 'Boss export India'?

Raku- It's a world class name. It is also universal I think we should finalize this as we can't get anything better than this. I will apply for it tomorrow and for export license too.

K.K- Yes sure. How much is the export license going to cost, 10-20,000 or more?

Raku- Brother it will cost 10-20,000 if you take the help of mediators. I checked on YouTube the fee is only 500 and also, we don't have to go anywhere because we can apply online.

K.K- Really, it's that easy? I thought it's going to cost a lot of money to gain an export license. It's cheaper than getting a driving license. In today's time it takes at least 2000 rupees for getting a driving license. You should apply for it by god's grace.

Raku- Ok Boss.

K.K- I am not your boss please call me brother. You can call boss to your wife after you get married. She will only tell you who is a Boss.

Raku- You have not even gotten married, my turn is quite late. You should get married now as you are well settled. With good name and work you have everything.

K.K- Surely I will get married too, but right now my focus is on my work. My goal is to see my business reach great heights. Right now our work is only limited to one district I want to take it to a world class level. I want the whole world to talk about us.

Raku- Surely the world will talk about us, we will work very hard.

Next day raku's father stormed into my house

Where is the K.K! come out! Why are you hell bent on ruining my son??

What have we done to you?

K.K- why are you shouting so loudly who has Ruined whom?

Raku's father- look K.K we are simple people. Neither do we have money to run a business. I thought that I will educate my son so that he will become an officer or a manager. But I don't know how you coaxed him in your talks. Now he says that he will do business that too by exporting. You do whatever you want but leave my son out of it we are simple people and we know our place very well. Why are you involving my boy in your business? If tomorrow you incur a loss of 10- 20 lacs you will make us sell our house.

K.K- Kaka he came by his own will in this business. And about the money, who has asked you any money?I have just asked him to work with me, if there is a loss, I will handle it I will never come to you asking for money. He is just a partner in profit not in losses.

Kaka- I will not come in your talks I just want my son to secure a government job so that he can live a peaceful life. There is no stability in business. Export business is not for small people like us. If my son gets stuck who will be answerable? You are clever you can pave your way out of any situation but Raku is young.

K.K- you don't know the worth of your son, he is a diamond. Don't worry at all just trust the Gods plan and everything will be alright.

Kaka -we are very small people buy lots of hard work have we completed his education. I will give you both one year, If something substantial happens in one year then you can continue, if not then he will prepare for a government job.

K.K- thank you so much for giving us the time and showing faith in us. We will never let you regret this decision.

And then he went back to his home

I did not think there was any fault in raku's father's thinking as he was correct in his own place. Our brains are so deeply stricken by this vicious circle of poverty that it does not give us any chance to try something new. And if somebody dares to try, people and the society stops him. Everybody is running to secure a government job. Big business is only left for big businessman. Small people do not even think about business and the blame for this goes to our education system it teaches us how to become a manager not a........

Our education system makes us a job finder not a job provider. And our government also has never thought about it. In Europe and America by the time a student graduates he has tried his hands in at least three businesses.

Their emphasis is more on learning rather than being successfulunsuccessful. Here we term failure as a huge thing.

After failing once we never try again and if somebody tries, again the society tags him as a failure and reminds him daily about prior failures, till their courage is broken.

The people should learn from their failures as they showcase the mistakes done earlier which helps in in showing the person, the correct way for succeeding.

But from several years, slavery has come in our DNA. Thinking of just securing jobs is a symbol of that slavery. Securing just a 20k govt job is enough for marriage proposals to line up, but if the boy goes in private for a 50k salary, the proposals will never come. My goal is not to provide jobs but to prepare thousands of K.K's like me so that they can help in making our economy strong. So that our nation can stop the tyranny of a handful of wealthy families.

Help myself and people like me, but you can only help the other person if you are capable yourself. The company was started that from a small room with only a cupboard and a table with the laptop on it. This was our small office which was actually a room in Rakesh's house. The advantage of having and of this in your own house was that you can start and end the work whenever you feel like. A person can work freely and the working hours can also increase.

Firstly, we have to select the list of projects for export. We shortlisted the easily available products found in our area which included agriculture products, furniture, handicraft, mobile, granite and several other kinds of stones.

Apart from this several minerals were included in the list like gypsum, limestone, calcium powder etc

So, we curated a long list and we thought of dealing with all of these products. It was time to live the dreams. The job of finding the buyers for export was given to Rakesh who from morning to evening mailed to different companies worldwide enquiring about their raw material requirement.

He used to mail around a hundred messages to which approx. five replied.

And those five companies inquired about the rates, international graded and standards, we failed to give them a satisfactory reply as we did not have proper product knowledge.

Soon we knew one thing that we need to master the knowledge of one product and focus just on it. Just like how in a hunt if the Lion focuses on the whole pack of deer's he will sleep hungry but if he focuses on one and follows him only, then the prey will be hunted down.

So, I decided that I will choose one product. In the end the trade of stones was finalized which included marble granite and sandstone. We decided to just focus on this and started gaining lots of information from Marble and Granite factories. We gained lots of technical and product knowledge. Now with the help of Internet and social media sites we started our marketing.

When your name starts coming in the market then many export trade helping companies try to connect with you. One of these called me.

"Hello sir I am Shruti from export world.com can I talk to you for 10 minutes."

"Yes sure"

"Sir with our company's help you can get 10 to 50 genuine buyers monthly, who will be related to your product for that you have to take our membership which is divided into gold, silver and Platinum. The fee varies from 25k, 50k and 1 lakh per annum respectively.

I got coaxed in her talks and took a platinum membership and thought that now buyers will directly contact us. Because of this, three months went by but not even one order was confirmed. I understood quickly that the scope of our product is not much online.

K.K- Raku it has been four months and we still have not got even one order we are doing something wrong.

Raku- yes brother, this will not work we should change our tactics.

K.K- I think we should connect with the original buyer directly. If the buyer is in front of us, the chances of order confirmation increases. It all depends on our presentation and our convincing skills.

Raku- you are right brother, but why will any foreigner come to us in India and even if he comes, we don't have a factory or stock yard to show him.

K.K- customer will not come to us we will have to go to the customer.

R.K- do we have to go to foreign lands?

K.K- surely, we have to go. Our brand has not become famous that the foreigner's themselves will come to us. We have to go to them for the sale of our product.

R.K- this will cost a lot and what if we do not get orders.

K.K- the expenses will be there. Are you thinking that without spending the money, we'll get orders? We would have to spend on our travels. Even If the orders do not come, winning and losing is all in God's hand we just have to do hard work without caring about the results. We will not leave the field just for the fear of losing. We will fight till we become successful.

R.K - I feel confident after hearing you talk.

K.K- which country should we choose for marketing?

R.K- brother we should go to any country in US or Europe, as the trade of luxury goods is immense there.

K.K -these countries will not give us the visa right now. Choose the country that will easily give the Visa and from where we can find easy buyers too.

R.K- then we should choose Qatar as 2022 World Cup is going to be played there. There must be lots of construction work going on which well lead to increase in the consumption of our product.

K.K- OK then apply for the visa in Qatar and book the flight tickets. Our first target will be Qatar as we have more chances of getting orders from there.

The tickets were booked for the next month of August.

Raku- brother I will sit on the window seat of the plane as it's my first travel in the plane and also my first foreign trip.

K.K- Yes as if I travel daily in the plane this is my first time too, I will sit on the window seat while going to Qatar and you can sit while we return to India.

R.K- how long will be stay there?

K.K- Ten days are enough, book a hotel for 10 days.

Finally, that day arrived when we took our first business trip. In August there was monsoon season which is very pleasing.

Me and Raku packed new clothes for this trip and took flight from Delhi for our first ever flight.

Raku- brother this Delhi Airport is huge I think the flights from all over the world must go from here.

K.K -this is an international airport, the flights from all over the world come and go.

The flight took off on time and throughout the flight Rakesh kept uttering Hanuman Chalisa as he was scared. As soon as we went out, it felt like we had come near a hot furnace. Even in the evening the temperature was 45 degrees.

It was scorching hot.

We took our taxi and I went to the hotel straight away. Because we were so tired we thought of resting that night.

The next morning, we prepared ourselves at 6:00am for marketing of a product in an unknown City, of which we didn't know anything and the language and the culture was different too. No one was there to tell us directions but me managed.

We waited for 8 o'clock for the markets to open. With the help of Google we searched marble and granite shops nearby within 1-5 kilometer of our location. We thought of deciding to walk to visit the shops that were in the radius of 5 kms. As the time was increasing so was the heat and soon walking got very difficult for us at 9 a.m. itself the temperature reached 47 degrees. We had never witnessed such heat ever. Our bodies were soaked because of sweat and I had started feeling dizzy.

Somehow, we managed to go to the person that we wanted to meet. The owner of that showroom was an Irani. Initially we talked to him in English in whichever way we could and introduced ourselves and showed him the pictures of a product including the rates. He liked the pictures and the rates but he asked for a sample which we did not have. As the stones are heavy in weight, we thought that the pictures will do the trick.

They were demanding samples which was a normal rule of selling to the customer. If your product is good and the rates are also fine there will be a sale. Here the rates were also good but the samples were not with us. He told us to first show the sample only then he will give the order.

We told him that will courier him the samples and bid farewell.

Troubled by the heat, we booked a taxi for 7 days to go to the locations that we wanted. In 7 days, we visited more than 30 workshops.

Some people were not at all interested but one thing was confirmed that the sample is very important. Seeing the pictures will not do the trick.

On the 9th and the last day Raku was making a list of the reasons because of which the orders were not confirmed.

1. No availability of sample.

2. No availability of a catalogue.

3. Language related problems.

K.K- Raku we have to work on these three causes.

And as soon as we go to India, we have to find solutions for these three problems and prepare with twice as much energy and come back. And we will book the return ticket only when we will have the order.

Raku- Yes my brother we will surely come back.

Hence our first business trip failed badly. We did not succeed in our first attempt but as soon as we landed Rakesh's friend were waiting for us with questions like how many orders did you get or did you come back empty handed?

Raku- No nothing right now but we have hopes to get in future.

Them- why are you wasting your time. You should do a work which is of your level, you cannot become experts just like that. This is for big people it needs higher education and lots of investment which you do not have.

Look for a job.

At that time Rakesh kept quiet because he did not have any answer, but in the evening he told me all about it and said "Our maangilal was also making fun of me and making taunts."

K.K- listen Raku do not get demotivated by listening to their talks. What has he done in his life till now? The people who do not do anything themselves often hinder the ones who want to achieve something. It's the world's job to pull other people down. We have to show them by our work. I will prove to everyone that even village people can become big.

R.K- yes I know but..

K.K- but what? Just trust yourself I have too come out of this phase. I know what to do. Do not worry. Just plan for our next trip and get that brochure printed out meanwhile I will arrange the sample in 4-5 days. This time do not book the return ticket beforehand we will only come back after the order is confirmed.

R.K- yes brother we will prepare with twice much energy and we will get the order confirmed.

K.K -Raku we are new for these people, that's why they will not give us advance payment. So, we have to give all our material on credit.

R.K- but brother credit that too in a foreign land. What if the payments are stuck?

K.K- we will take the risk but not with closed eyes.

R.K- I do not understand brother.

K.K- we will make some rules and Standards to give credit whoever will fare well on these rules, we will give them the material and not to everyone.

R.K- how will we set the standards for whom to give and not?

K.K - a person's upkeep can tell a lot about their economic conditions. We will visit their showroom and warehouse for that. If a person has a material of hundred crores, he will not get greedy for our 8 to 10 lakh rupees. And here many workers are Indian or Bengali, we will ask them about their owner. The one who takes care of the workers means that party is solid, we can surely give them the material on credit. And also, the reputation in the market about a person will tell a lot about them. If somebody has a bad reputation in the market, we will get to know about it before hand

And the last option is to see their account statement of last one year which is issued by bank. It will show their turnover and also whether any cheque has been dishonored. In this way we will be able to check their financial conditions. We will keep these things in mind then chances of payment to be received will be 99%.

R.K- wow brother, from where did you get such divine knowledge, I also want to learn these things.

K.K- No University of the world or any book on will be able to tell you these solutions, I have learnt these experiences after researching the causes of incurring several losses of lacs of rupees. We have good product which has a good demand in the market. But there are several suppliers who will not let us enter this market easily because we are new, therefore we need to put credit in our plan.

R.K- but brother this will increase our installment how will we arrange so much money?

K.K- for that we will go to the bank.

In today's time government is funding several startups we will take help from the bank just like several big business groups take loans from the banks of huge amount of money. Now you prepare, for us to go to Qatar I don't want to come back empty handed again.

R.K- I have booked the tickets for the 5th of October. Also, in October the heat is a little less.

K.K- yes good then, I will prepare some catalogue and samples. There shouldn't be a lack of presentation this time.

Finally, that day came when we took the flight of Qatar again. This time our preparation was complete and we had already texted our last time driver Ashok. He came to pick us on time at the airport.

As soon as we got out of the airport, he greeted us.

Ashok- welcome back in Qatar your driver is here for you sir.

K.K- don't joke Ashok please take us to the hotel fast.

Ashok- for how many days are you going to stay this time?

K.K- At least one month or more.

Ashok- are you planning on settling here?

K.K- no but this time we will not return empty handed. You have to stay with us for a long time now till we are here in Qatar. If you know any translator of Arabic, please tell me we need a translator.

Ashok- what are you saying I have been in Qatar since the last 10 years you will not find a better translator than me.

K.K- perfect then, you will accompany us in every meeting with the client atranslator. How much will you charge for it?

Ashok- you can pay me whatever you wish by your own will for this. I just need the rent for my cab.

K.K- let's do one thing, Whichever orders will be confirmed by the translator you will get 10% from the profit. We were so busy in our talks, the hotel has arrived let's rest for now. Pick us up tomorrow morning at 8 o'clock ok bye.

R.K- brother the whole list is ready. We have to target these people. We will have a meeting with 5 companies today, I have mailed everyone and all have approved the appointments.

K.K- very good. Ashok must be waiting for us let's go in the lobby downstairs.

Ashok- welcome boss I am ready to serve you please tell me where to take you?

R.K- today we have to go to the Al-Wakhra Road we will visit all the showrooms there.

Ashok- ok but I have to check the car break a letter so can we go to the car workshop first?

K.K- ok sure. We are not in a hurry, we can go to the Mechanics to check the brakes first.

Ashok at the workshop

"Brother the brakes are a little slow in the car please check".

After a while mechanic.

"Please check now they will feel like magnets on the road now".

"We call Abdul Bhai a magician, the cars run smooth as silk when he touches them."

K.K -Abdul Bhai what do you do with this black oil which comes out of the vehicles when you change the oil?

Abdul Bhai- it's a huge headache we have to give 50 Riyals only to get this picked up.

Almost 1000 rupees of India only to get rid of this.

K.K- In India a drum of the black oil is sold at 7000 but they give us the money to pick it up. You will earn great profit, if you send this to India. For me it is black gold.

R.K -if we will import the black oil in India, we will have to give so muchduty and custom on it.

K.K- Raku it's going to take five minutes to check on the net.

R.K- brother in Qatar import duties are 20% and 18% GST so total 38%.

K.K -still it will get double after going to India.

To Abdul Bhai- who takes this black oil away, here do you have his number?

Abdul- yes sure, his name is Saddam. Here is his number (and he handed over the number).

Now we were on Ryan Road

K.K to Ashok- take us to Mr. Saddam.

Ashok- But we were going to the marble granite dealer.

K.K- We will go to him later first take us to Saddam's address.

Ashok- ok sir.

After a while at Saddam warehouse

"We want to meet Mr. Saddam tell them a party has come to meet from India, this is our card."

Watchman- Please wait I will come in 2 minutes.

After a while

Watchman- you can come inside. Saddam sir's office is in room number 7.

After thanking the guard we walked towards room number 7.

Inside the room

Mr. Saddam was a healthy man who was originally from Afghanistan. In the room we three introduced ourselves and told him the cause of our meeting.

Saddam- we will give you the material in whatever quantity you want but the rate will be 100 dirhams for one drum. If you agree with the rates, you can deposit the advance.

K.K- brother I will take 5000 drums per month from you so give the rates accordingly.

Saddam's eyes started sparkling as soon as he heard 5,000 drums.

Saddam- for 5000 drums I can lessen 10 dirhams for you, you can close the deal.

K.K- brother keep it 80 dirhams .we will surely buy in large quantity from you once we are in business together.

Saddam- ok let's finalize it at 85 and then you can give the advance. I will give you to the name of the port and get it delivered next month.

K.K- give us your account number and then we will transfer the payment from India.

Saddam- I will WhatsApp you my account details.

K.K- thanks a lot Mr. Saddam see you soon.

After saying this we left the room.

I called Mr. Sunil the oil dealer in India as soon as I sat in my car.

K.K- Namaste Sunil Seth.

Sunil- Namaste K.K brother, you are calling from a foreign number where are you enjoying?

K.K - There are people like you who enjoy brother, we are only searching for work here. Is there any demand for black oil?

Sunil- what rate will you give and how much quantity?

K.K- I can provide you 5000 drums every month. For 7000rs per drum. The oil is of great quality.

Sunil- Keep it at 6800 per drum and send me.

K.K- But you have to make the advance payment.

Sunil- ok but only 25%. Send me your account number I will transfer it today.

K.K- Ok I am sending you the account details; the oil will reach you in 20 days. Total amount will be 3 Crore 40 lacs. Transfer the 25% of this. I will call you when I come back to India.

K.K To R.K- How much will it cost per drum to us.

R.K- brother it will cost around 2000 rupees and 1600 for transit so it will cost a total of Rs 3600.

K.K- So that means this deal will give a profit of about 1 crore 40 lacs. Arrange the return flight to India. Now we will sell black oil because it has more profit.

R.K- And what about marble granite?

K.K- You stay here for that and do Marketing for it. I will go back to India and set the market for black oil. It is the first time that we have got such a huge deal. The rule of the sales is simple if your rate and product has potential and quality then your product will sell and here are both the things are perfect. Let me catch the first flight to India.

R.K- What will I do here alone?

K.K- You will help Saddam bhai in getting the oil loaded. I don't trust these people, what if they sent water instead of oil. We will lose our money.

R.K- No no, I will take care of it. You go back to India I will see the work here.

Next day

I returned to India. As soon as I landed, I activated my Indian number. I got a call from an unknown number when I picked up, a girl in a sweet voice said to me in English "Am I talking to Mr. K.K of Boss export?"

I said, "Yes, I am Vikas tell me mam how can I help you?"

"Sir our company will provide you data regarding export for six months."

K.K- What will happen by that? I had understood these people were just the spies of the international Interpol who........

Madam- this will help you in in trading we will tell you about .... and provide details about.....

K.K- Ok send me the data of last six months of China regarding marble and Granite.

Madam- We are not spies sir, we can only provide you the data of India not of other countries.

K.K- mam can I ask you a personal question if you do not mind.

Madam- sure why not.

K.K- what's your age and do you have a boyfriend?

Madam- I am 22 and yes, I do but why are you asking this?

K.K- ok how did you interact with him for the very first time on phone or face to face?

Madam- no he was with me in college.

K.K- did you propose for him?

Madam- no it took 6 months for him to convince me.

K.K- that's the similarity between convincing a customer and a girl. If he had proposed you then and there on a call and you haven't seen him face to face would you have accepted his proposal?

Madam- no not at all.

K.K- The thing is, that you are providing me the number of the girl and asking me to propose to her. In my experience there is only a 2% chance to convince a customer on phone or mail. But if you sit on a table with them the chance increases to a 50%. And already there is so much competition in India. If you want to give us a source then give to other Nations like China Turkey and Pakistan.

Here in India a person works so hard to earn money, from selling a product but people like you ruin their hard work. I don't deal in this kind of business as I have the capability of hunting for myself and not have to survive on other people's leftovers so, please do not call me again.

And I hung up.

An old man sitting beside me was hearing this whole conversation.

He asked me, "what do you do son?"

K.K- Uncle I deal with oil chemical and export.

Uncle- can I get your card I also have an oil filter plant in Gurgaon.

K.K- black oil filter?

Uncle- Yes son.

K.K- I get black soil in huge quantity, you can take it from me if you want.

Uncle- call me tomorrow. I got impressed by your conversation with that Call Centre girl. This is my card keep it with you and email me your rates.

K.K- sure sir, thank you I will email you all the details. Now I have to go to Terminal two. I am in a hurry or else I will miss my flight.

I took my luggage after saying this and hurried to the domestic airport. In the flight itself I compiled the rates and sent it on the given email ID. After two days his reply came and also an offer of 10000 drums. Now I had an order of 15000 drums to be provided to both the companies every month.

Earning 5 to 6 crores profit every month was a huge opportunity for me. In Qatar, Raku had also gotten a big Jackpot. Our company got a contract of supplying marble and granite to three big stadiums which was an order of 150 million. In 3-4 months, money started raining in. In the end of the year our company's turnover was 100 crores.

Now my next target was to import black oil from foreign Nations and filter it myself. I set up the biggest black oil filter refinery of India and started producing new oil from the old and exporting it back to foreign Nations.

In Qatar the granite orders were also increasing. There is a saying that money attracts money. In India I was named the oil king and in just two years, our company became one of the top 5 companies in oil and Granite industry in India.

We were increasing the business day by day and had opened more than thousand marble and Granite dealerships in in more than 120 nations. We were employing more than 100 thousand people.

On that day my mother's wish came true that it I don't have to get a job I will provide jobs. It had been five years.

Miss Neha- Sir your life has been an interesting journey. Now you have achieved all your dreams what do you think about marriage?

K.K- I haven't found my miss right yet. But you will surely hear the good news after ICL. My mother has found a girl for me.

Neha- you will do arrange marriage? you did not fall in love with anyone?

K.K- My first love is cricket because of that I am here. Marriage is a social bond which everyone should have. But I had married my work

Neha- Still your office is in your village, all multinational companies have their offices in cities. You still operate from here is there any special reason?

K.K- No I do have offices in metro cities but I love my village. And my mother is also here, that's why our head office is in this village. Ok now I have to go in an urgent meeting. It was a pleasure talking to you. Please print this interview as it is, without any edits.

Neha- thank you so much for your time.

Next day

R.K- brother RT camp is going to start from Monday which will continue for a month. You have to join it too.

K.K- Till then you will see all my important works and other meetings for two months. I just want to focus on my game. I will work hard in the nets for at least a month.

SS stadium Jaipur

Coach Joshi introduced all the team members. Joshi in team meeting.

"As you all know the owner of RT is Mr. K.K and he will be captaining the team this time"

Viraj Kohli smiling.

"So, we should forget about the ICL cup."

"Joshi sir do you know what you are saying?"

Joshi- I have taken this decision carefully. If Mr. K.K fails in any field in the nets in front of you, he will quit himself. I have taken his fitness test. This is about standards I hope you are all ready for the practice.

(All the boys go in the nets)

Joshi to K.K- you should show all the boys what you are capable of. Wear the pads and be ready I will ask Jofra to bowl.

Joshi to Viraj- According to you in how many sixes on Jofra's bowling will you admit that K.K is an international player.

Viraj- I also get tensed while Jofra bowls. It's impossible, he cannot do it.

In the nets Jofra in front of K.K who is famous for his killer bouncers and Yorkers. Mr K.K batting with left hand and taking guard on the off stump.

Joshi- Ready? start bowling Jofra.

Jofra took his run up, the very first ball was a bouncer that struck straight on the helmet.

K.K checked his helmet and Viraj's voice is heard, "Bowl slowly if it struck on his head, the team will be shot of the captain".

K.K- no ball in your own rhythm don't worry.

Next ball was on the same line but this time on leg side, with the pull shot the ball was hit for a 6. The third ball was a middle stump yorker he played it making a little room on the left side, behind the wicket for four runs. The next ball was a good length on which K.K hit a straight six.

Sixteen runs were scored in just 4 balls. Till the over completed, 24 runs were scored which was a very good strike rate in T20 cricket.

The next over was of off spin bowler Vikas Yadav who has good experience in international cricket. But this time K.K was bathing with his right hand.

Joshi- Are you left-handed or right-handed?

K.K- that you can decide yourself.

He hit three sixes in Vikas's over. Yadav and Viraj Kohli exclaimed, "what a man he is. On both sides same footwork, same cover drive, same straight drive. It's difficult to tell whether is left hand is good or right hand."

Everyone in the team was impressed with his batting and bowling. K.K's batting was decided by looking at the bowler, whether he will play with right or left hand. After a month of practice sessions, the day came when the tournament was inaugurated.

K.K was in the headlines even before the inauguration. Newspapers and cricket analysts were commenting upon him. Some cricket experts were saying that K.Ks captaincy was gained by money and power. The opposition team I was talking about defeating them in the very first round. The betting markets was also providing the lowest rate for RT. Overall, the whole l environment was against the RT team.

Before the first match for the press conference, the captain himself was present in the meeting hall.

Journalist- should we call you business tycoon K.K or the player K.K?

K.K- I am the player K.K in front of you, as I am out of the business arena.

Journalist- With which capabilities do you dare to say that ICL Cup will be won by your team?

K.K- Our team is a mixture of youth and experience. We are not just daring to say we are pretty confident of winning it.

Journalist- I hope this is not your overconfidence, as even the captain of the team doesn't have any experience of domestic or international cricket.

K.K- I will answer this with my game tomorrow. You will know it in tomorrow's match with my bat,

Journalist- I hope you are not a prey of over self-confidence.

K.K- I can do it is my self-confidence and only I can do it is overconfidence. It's up to you what you think. I do not care. Thank you.

The Press Conference ends.

Then next day:

The stadium was packed and all the tickets were booked a week before the match.

Before the match

K.K- Raku what is my rate in the betting market?

R.K (laughing)- brother why will anyone put money on you. The rate is 20 for 1, for your man of the match.

K.K- do one thing put 10 lacs on me.

R.K- brother I don't want to lose my money it's your first match. Will see in the next match.

K.K- do whatever I have asked you to do, just trust me.

It's time for the toss and he went on the ground

Commentator- Greetings everybody on this mega match. Today's match is being played between Rajasthan Tigers in Delhi lions. Both the captains are present in the ground and the toss is being held now.

The toss is won by Delhi lions captain Venugopal and he has opted for fielding. The captain K.K of RT is invited to bat first.

For viewers information I want to tell you that the captain and the owner of this team both is Mr. K.K. Which has happened for the very first time in sport's history. Its hasn't even happened in football, basketball or in any other sport .

The opening pair of RT has come on the ground. Sheikh Nawab is on strike and Mr. K.K on non-striker's end.

The first ball was being bowled by Ross Tydler who is the renowned fast bowler of Australia. On strike is Nawab facing

Ross. The first ball was pushed towards mid-on, played with light hands for one run.

Now K.K is on strike who is playing his first ever match of ICL, who will face the second ball of the over. It struck straight on the helmet after bouncing. It was quite fast which struck right below the eye and he started bleeding. The stretcher came in the ground but K.K refused to go from the ground. The physio explained that the cut is deep and it will require stitches.

K.K- just bandage it right here. I will play.

Commentator 1- the players should know their capabilities. Not anyone should be sent with a bat in their hands in such big events.

Commentator 2- yes Harshad you are right. Any amateur shouldn't be allowed to play just because of their money. But what is this, K.K is returning to the ground. He will face Ross Tydler once again!

The third over of the ball was again a bouncer. This time by the pull shot on the leg side, was struck for six runs outside the boundary. The next ball was of good length. Played above the covers for one more six!!

The next ball was played on the packet above the slip for four runs. On the last ball, cut slowly on the Gully for one run and kept the strike.

In the end of the over,

1, 0, 6, 6, 4, 1 with a total of 18 runs.

Commentator 1 - he hits the ball good with great timing.

Commentator 2 -It's too soon to say as the whole match is left. The next over is of spin by Rashid.

But K.K is now batting from his left hand against this leg spinner. He played the ball slowly with the pull shot.

Commentator- what is he doing. Playing with left and right both hands.

On the next ball he hit a six above the mid-on with the spin and gave everybody the proof that his left hand was equally well like the right hand. In the eighth over of the match he got out after making 77 runs with 8 sixes and 7 fours. The total score of the team was 185.

Now it was time for them to bowl which was also headed by K.K.

Commentator- To bowl the very first over is K.K right arm over the Wicket.

The first ball was a leg cutter which was caught straight by the keeper, missing the bat, with the speed of 138km/hr. The batsman was completely clueless with both speed and swing deadly.

The next ball pitched on the middle and straight away struck on the wickets from the gap between bat and the pad. Clean bowled!

K.K had made a breakthrough taking the wicket in the very first over. This time the ball swinged on the inside and the batsman failed completely to read the line of the ball therefore giving away his wicket.

The new batsman in was Rahul Rai. With K.K bowling right arm over the wicket , a deadly yorker struck straight on the middle stump and left it flying.

Commentator- Two wickets in 2 balls. What is happening harsh?? Is this really his debut match!!

"What a performance.First in batting and now in bowling. Just see his confidence which can be seen in his body language.

The next batsman in will be Chris facing K.K. With K.K on a hattrick. Coming with a slow runup, right arm over the wicket ball, struck straight on the pads in front of the wicket. A string appeal for lbw.

"What has happened and umpire has raised his finger. OUT!!" The whole team picked up K.K and the whole stadium was chanting "K.K, K.K...."

"What a performance. A magical performance in his debut match with both batting and bowling has never happened ever in the cricketing history that too with a player who had never played an international or even a domestic match at any level."

RT winning their first match with 130 runs. K.K performed brilliantly took 6 wickets. And was awarded man of the match

Journalist- what do you want to say about your performance today?

K.K- I just played my natural game that's it. And just applied all my cricketing skills.

Journalist- this was your first match and you played like you have been practicing a lot.

K.K - the other teams should get nervous after seeing our performance. Our preparation is complete.

Journalist- who coached you in cricket?

K.K- the biggest coach is your own self. Whatever I did was only because of my skills and the practice I did.

Journalist- you are the senior most player in this tournament. Do you have a message for the younger players?

K.K- don't ever give up because of difficult circumstances. Keep dreaming and work very hard to achieve them. Don't ever blame the difficulties as everyone has to fight their own battles. Thankyou now I have to go to the team meeting.

In the hotel room:

R.K- brother, what a great match. I have earned great profits on the bet placed on you on the very first match.

K.K- I told you to trust me. I have never traded in losses. Earnings of 5000 crores on the very first match!

Transfer the 1100 crores from the betting money into our Mauritius and Dubai account. Give all the leftover amount in charity as you know how much curse it comes with. We just had to cover our loss that we took in buying the 1100 crore team. Put the remaining money in boss charitable trust. There is a great power in the prayers of poor people.

And you know we have achieved this much only because of prayers. The money feels good only at a limit because at the end you just need 2 meals a day to live. We have to earn for ourselves but we should give back to the society too. That's why we should earn more.

R.K- so when did I say no. Give charity all you want but just get married now. So that it's my turn. I am tired of being in casual relationships.

I have fallen in love with 20 girls before. I want to get married to this 21st one now. So please get married.

K.K- when have I stopped you?

R.K- how can a younger brother get married while his older brother is still a bachelor?

K.K- you are getting crazy. Get off my back. Let me first meet an appropriate girl.

R.K- already there had been a long list of girls wanting to marry you but now after tonight's match, the whole of India will have huge lines.

K.K-of whom?

R.K- of my future sister in law's. You have achieved your goal, at least now break this vow.

K.K (dismissively)- you just finalize that Nigerian deal of gold mines. We have to make the mining minister's daughter a partner of 25 percent in it. He has finally agreed.

R.K (angrily) just money money, this deal that deal. Our whole life is going to end in these deals. I also have some wishes of having 4-5 nephew nieces who will call me "chachu lets play cricket. When will that day come?"

K.K- you have started again. I have to go for my practice.

(He picked up his cricket kit and left)

He kept on performing outstandingly in all the matches and went on to acquire both the golden ball and bat. No other player could come even close to his performance.

All old records had been broken.

The team's in the final of ICL were Rajasthan tigers and Bengal bulls.

At the finals

Commentator- what a fantastic journey has it been. The Rajasthan tigers and their captain has proved that with passion and hunger you can conquer anything.

Agar ji- nobody thought that he will perform like this in this age. He has set a fine example for youngsters.

Harsh- K.K with a bat is equivalent to hanuman ji with his mace who is all-time ready to smash the bowlers and the ball like Sudarshan chakra going at electric speed once left from his hand. Nobody even came close to performing like K.K in the whole tournament.

It's the first time in ICL history that RT has reached the finals with the help of such a player who is an unknown star of the cricketing world.

Agar- I think he has some superhuman powers. How can a person be so perfect?

On the final match all the prior players, coaches and staff of Rajasthan tigers was invited. Among them was that person too who demanded 15 lakhs of bribe from K.K 25 years back.

K.K asked a staff member to call the retired selector Mr. Prakash into the dressing room.

Mr. Prakash was now a 70-year-old man.

"Mr. Prakash you are summoned to the dressing room."

Prakash- by whom?

Staff- Mr. K.K.

Prakash- ok I am coming.

As soon as he entered the dressing room K.K touched his feet.

Prakash- what are you doing. You are really a man of great skill. You have stirred up the cricket world. Praise to the mother who gave birth to such a star. I am your big fan.

K.K signaled all the players to leave them alone.

K.K- I want to talk to Mr. Prakash alone. Please wait for us in the lobby.

Everyone leaves

K.K- you are the inspiration behind all my achievements.

Prakash- I don't understand. What are you saying?

K.K- try to remember my face.

Prakash- no I am meeting you for the first time. I am not understanding what you are trying to say?

K.K- Twenty-five years ago from today, you were the head of the selection committee of RT.

Prakash- Yes I was.

K.K- A lean boy came to you whom you selected in the top 20. But you demanded 15 lakhs to take him in the team.

Blood drained out of his face as soon as he heard this.

K.K- I was that boy whom you kicked out even though I had the skills.

Prakash- son I am ashamed of what I did.

K.K- no I wanted to thank you. If you'd have given me a chance that day, only I'd have benefited But because of your decision millions of people are benefiting. Today because of my company I am able to provide for many. Whatever happens, happens for a reason. Whatever I have achieved till now is because of me not getting selected that day.

Prakash- I am really regretful for that day.

K.K- no Mr. Prakash. God had planned something even greater for me that why you rejected me. I told you all this alone because I don't want a scandalous situation for you.

Prakash- you have a huge heart Mr. K.K. All my prayers are with you.

K.K- now it's time for toss. Give me your blessings.

Prakash- (teary eyed) you are a magician. You have stolen my heart what more blessings shall I give you. You are a blessing yourself.

K.K -thankyou sir.

Left for the toss

Commentator- captain of both the teams are present here for the toss

And the toss has won by Bengal bulls captain Amit Rahane, he has chosen to bat after winning the toss. RT will field against the Bengal Bulls.

Opening players have come into the ground. It has been an incredible journey in the tournament for Bengal Bulls.

But RT have been in another league altogether winning all their matches like knockouts.

The first over of RT being bowled by the captain himself.

The first ball being bowled right arm over the Wicket defended well by the batsman. The next ball on the offside batsman leaving it and straight into the keepers' gloves. Well defended again.

The whole over was maiden.

Commentator- I think the players of Bengal do not want to take any chances in front of K.K

The score in the second over.

6, 4, 4, 4, 1, 6

The strategy of the players was clear to defense against K.K and attack against the other bowlers. This strategy worked well for them and they scored 210 runs in 2o overs.

Now for the run chase opening pair of RT was in the ground. On strike was K.K and Viraj Kohli on the non-striker's end. They need an average of 10.5 runs per over to win this match.

The first ball will be faced by K.K, played with soft hands and stole one run.

Now on strike is Viraj, a fantastic cover drive on the second ball fetching him four runs. Left the next ball straight into the keepers' gloves. At the end of the first over the score was 9 runs. The opening pair batting brilliantly.

In five overs 60 Runs were scored without losing a wicket. In the next over, Viraj played a shot near the covers.

Commentator- played near the covers by Viraj, running for a run, fielder catching the ball and threw the ball targeting K.K and not the stumps. The ball struck him straight near the elbow.

"And K.K has lost his grip on the bat. He is writhing in pain."

Physio team coming into the ground.

Physio- it is swelling. You need to be treated.

K.K- just put an injection I can't leave the ground.

Physio- sir the condition is quite serious. You have to come out you can't even hold the bat with your right hand.

K.K- okay then send the next batsman in.

K.K was 'retire hurt' and left the ground, going to nearest hospital.

Doctor- your elbow is fractured. You won't be able to play cricket for at least 6 months.

K.K- doctor just give me an injection to curb the pain, my team needs me.

Dr-but you can't even pick the bat from your right hand.

K.K-don't worry my left hand is fine.

In the stadium wickets were tumbling one by one after K.K left the ground. Till returning to the ground the team had lost 7 wickets in 17 over scoring 160 runs. At the end of 18th over the team scored 174 runs and 2 more wickets making it 9 wickets overall.

Commentator- RT is in bad spot. Their chances of winning are gone. But look retired hurt K.K is coming back into the ground with a bandage around his right elbow.

As soon as he entered the stadium the crowd started chanting K.K... K.K

Commentator- all praises for K.K as he has stolen all our hearts no matter who wins the game. K.K will be on strike but will he bat with the left hand?

34 runs are needed in 9 balls to win this match. Facing the fourth wall of the over, a straight six!

"What a beautiful shot, that too with the left hand. He has tremendous power in his left hand".

The next ball was a short pitch bouncer, which he cut, above the keeper for 4 runs.

"What a start, he has bought back the match to life, wonderful!"

Last ball was pushed with light hands for one run, but because of misfield on the offside, went for 4 runs. But because of this four on strike will be the weaker batsman while K.K on the non-striker's end.

K.K to batsman- just run as soon as you touch the ball. You have to run even if you don't make contact.

First ball of the last over-

Batsman pushed the ball slowly on the leg side, and completed the run fast.

Now K.K on the striker's end. 19 runs in 5 balls are needed to win.

The first ball straight in the block hole. No run.

The match in a nail-biting position with 19 runs to be scored in just 4 balls.

The next ball was hit straight for a six. Ball vanishing into the dressing room.

The 3rd ball, short of length, played brilliantly on the off side for a six. Now only 2 balls remaining and 9 runs needed still.

The 4th ball: in an attempt of bowling a yorker, came straight onto the bat, struck out of the field for 4 runs.

The match has completely turned and K.K has shown the magic of his left hand. "What am astounding batting."

The last ball of the match- 5 runs to win. All eyes are on K.K.

K.K's eyes are on the ball.

A slow delivery but came on the center of the bat after pitching. The ball flying into the sky for a six!!

And Rajasthan Tigers has won the ICL cup for the very first time.

What a brilliant knock, with a broken hand this player turned a losing match into a winning one!

The end.
Part-2 Coming soon.

www.ingramcontent.com/pod-product-compliance
Lightning Source LLC
LaVergne TN
LVHW061344080526
838199LV00094B/7357